This book, the first that I've both written and illustrated, is dedicated to my parents. While neither were artists, they somehow managed to always provide sketchbooks, pencils, and paints along with their unwavering support for my love of drawing. I like to think they would be smiling to see the joyful life and career their encouragement has given me. Thank you, Mom and Dad.

Farrar Straus Giroux Books for Young Readers
An imprint of Macmillan Publishing Group, LLC
120 Broadway, New York, NY 10271 • mackids.com

Our books may be purchased in bulk for promotional, educational,
or business use. Please contact your local bookseller or the
Macmillan Corporate and Premium Sales Department at (800) 221-7945 ext. 5442
or by email at MacmillanSpecialMarkets@macmillan.com.

Library of Congress Cataloging-in-Publication Data
Names: Walker, David, 1965– author.
Title: Here with me / David Walker.
Description: First edition. | New York: FSG Books for Young Readers, 2022. |
Audience: Ages 3–6. | Audience: Grades K–1. |
Summary: A child concludes that the best place to be is together with one's parent.
Identifiers: LCCN 2021044582 | ISBN 9780374389291 (hardcover)
Subjects: CYAC: Stories in rhyme. | Parent and child—Fiction. |
Animals—Fiction. | Imagination—Fiction. |
LCGFT: Picture books. | Stories in rhyme.
Classification: LCC PZ8.3.W1513 He 2022 | DDC [E]—dc23
LC record available at https://lccn.loc.gov/2021044582

First edition, 2022
Book design by Elynn Cohen
Color separations by Bright Arts (H.K.) Ltd.
Printed in China by Toppan Leefung Printing Ltd., Dongguan City, Guangdong Province

ISBN 978-0-374-38929-1 (hardcover)
1 3 5 7 9 10 8 6 4 2

David Walker

Here with Me

Farrar Straus Giroux

New York

Sometimes I sit and wonder
who I would choose to be
if I could wish a wish
to be a different kind of me.

If I were a fox
with a tail fluffy red,
I'd bounce through the forest
till it was time for bed.

Or if I were a bear
all covered in fur,
I'd be big and scary
with my *grrr, grrr, grrr*!

Maybe I'd be a mouse,
so I could *squeak, squeak, squeak*.
And on my little feet
I would sneak, sneak, sneak.

Though if I had a choice
of just who I'd be,

I wouldn't change a thing,
so you'd be here with me.

But if . . .

. . . I were a sloth
moving slowly, slow, slow,
I could hang by my toes
everywhere I go.

I might choose a zebra.
Wouldn't that be fun?
I'd munch on the grass,
then I'd run, run, run!

Or I could be a bird,
singing all day,
till my beak got tired,
then I'd flap, flap away.

Though if I had a choice
of just who I'd be,

I wouldn't change a thing,
so you'd be here with me.

Buuuuuut if . . .

. . . I were a fish,
I would *splish-splash, bubble,*
and wiggle my tail
to get away from trouble.

Or I might pick a monkey,
silly as can be,
and I would climb and swing
in my banana tree!

But I would never choose
a different kind of me,
because right here with you
is where I want to be.

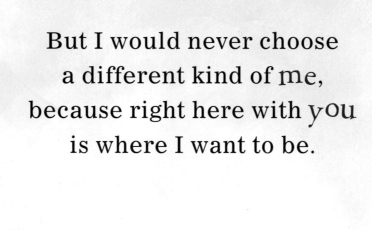